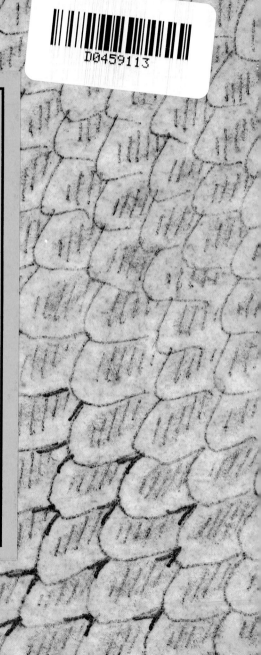

For Anna, Jan Niklas and Franziska Sophie

This edition is published and
distributed exclusively by
DISCOVERY TOYS Martinez, CA
Originally published by
Walker Books, Ltd, London

© 1988 John Talbot.
Printed in Hong Kong
First American Edition

ISBN 0-939979-11-X

The Dragon's Cold

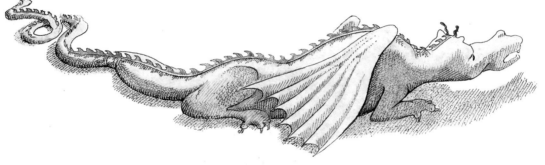

Written and illustrated by

John Talbot

DISCOVERY TOYS

"Come on!" called Alex.
He and his friends hurried down to the beach.

"Look at this," said Mimi. "Look what I've found!"

"It's very long," said Alex.

"And it's incredibly heavy," said Roland.
"What can it be?" asked Spike.

"It's a dragon!" they all shouted.
"Let's get out of here!"

"Oh, don't go," said the dragon.
"I won't hurt you." He sounded
very sad.

"What's the matter?" asked Mimi.

"It's this dreadful cold," sniffed the dragon. "It's completely put my fire out. All my family and friends sent me away. 'Duncan,' they said, 'no one wants a dragon without fire.'"

"We want you," said Mimi, "and we'll take care of you."

"We'll think of something," agreed Alex.

That very night, back in the village, all the sheets mysteriously disappeared from the clotheslines.

Next morning the villagers were very upset.
They asked Menzy, the local plumber, to stand
watch all night to catch the thieves.

"I'm really wasting my time," muttered Menzy. "I've got so much to do and there's still the town's old boiler to repair."

Then, as the moon came out, he saw an amazing sight.

"What are those kids up to?" he thought.

Menzy followed them back to the cave and watched
in astonishment. All night long the children sewed
the sheets together while the dragon, with his
runny nose, slept up on his ledge.

As the sun was rising, Menzy ran back to tell the villagers what he had seen.

"It was huge," he said.
"Oooooh, it must have been
as long as fifty lengths of pipe.
Come and see for yourselves."

From a safe distance they saw an incredible sight—
the children had made a huge handkerchief!

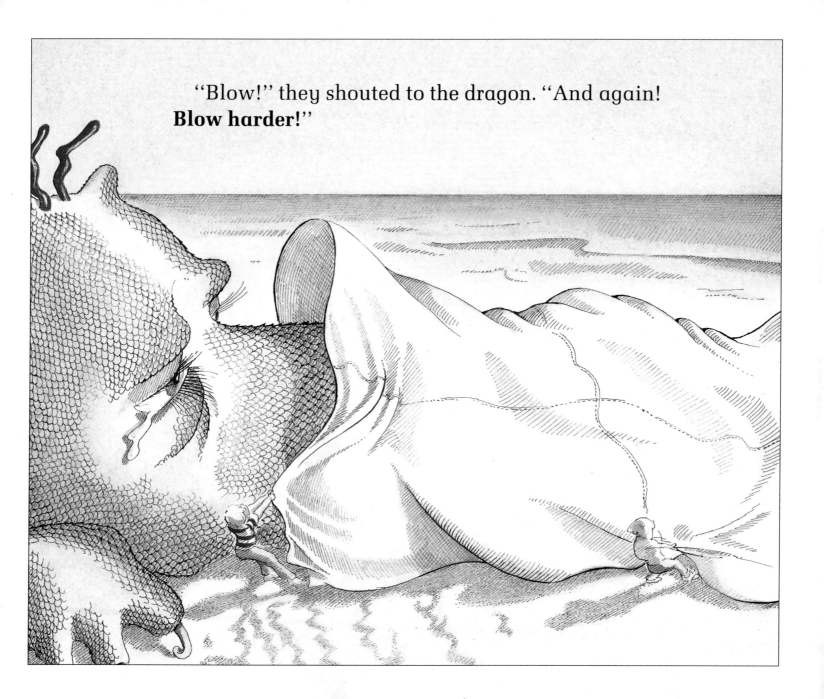

"Blow!" they shouted to the dragon. "And again! **Blow harder!**"

Whoosh!

Suddenly there was a loud roar of fire
as Duncan blew his nose.

"Oh my," he cried, "that's better! **Much better!**"

"Look, they're all running away!" shouted Spike.

"Come back, everyone," cried the others. "Duncan
won't hurt you. Come back!"

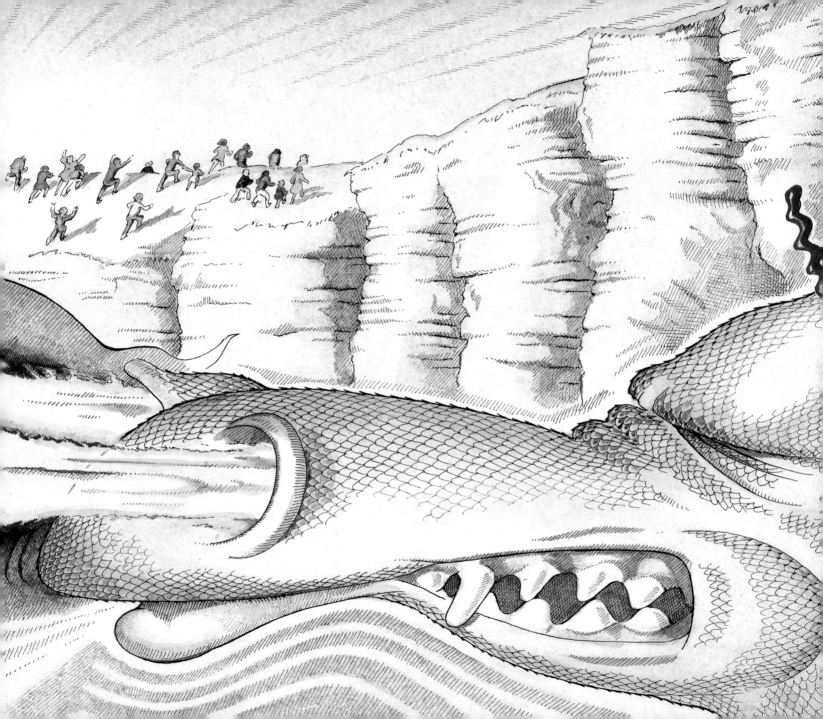

Slowly the villagers did come back, when they saw that the children weren't afraid.

"He's quite tame," said Mimi. "Look!" And she patted him on the tooth.

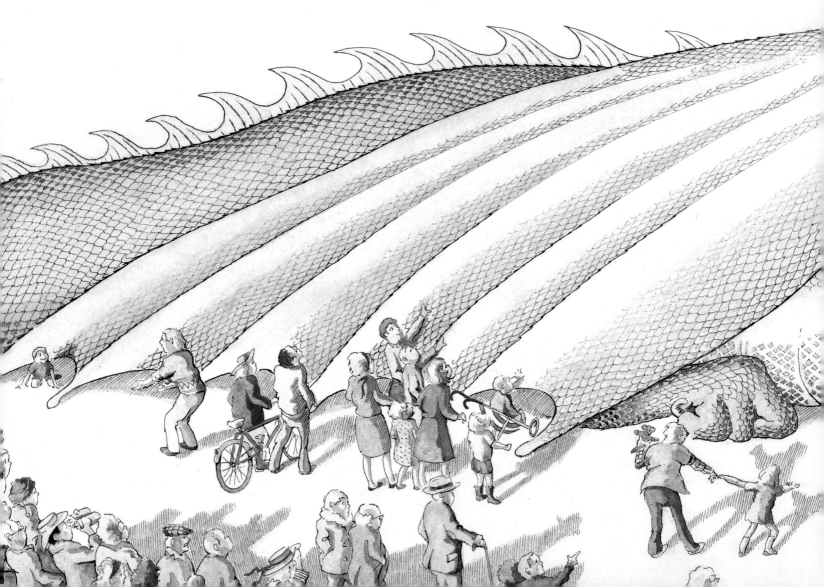

Duncan was so pleased to have his fire
back he decided to stay on and
live in his cave near the village.

"You've solved my problem with the old boiler,"
said Menzy.

So while the children prepared Duncan's breakfast,
the dragon provided piping hot water for the entire
village every morning.

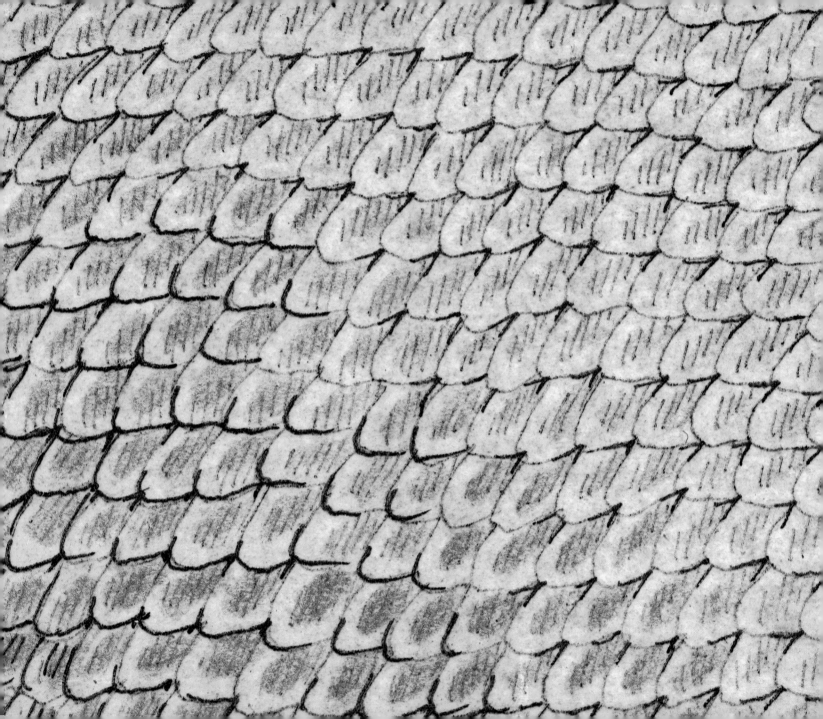